IN THE DARK

D0185268

Rigby, Halley Court, Jordan Hill, Oxford, OX2 8EJ
a division of Harcourt Education Ltd
www.myprimary.co.uk

Rigby is a registered trademark of Harcourt Education Ltd

In the Dark first published 2002

'Notre Dame of Paris' Adaptation © Steve Skidmore and Steve Barlow 2002
'The Hound of the Baskervilles' Adaptation © Steve Skidmore and Steve Barlow 2002
'Great Expectations' Adaptation © Michael Lawrence 2002

Series editor: Wendy Wren

06 05 04 03
10 9 8 7 6 5 4 3

| *In the Dark* | ISBN 0433 07854 5 |
| Group Reading Pack with Teaching Notes | ISBN 0433 07860 X |

Illustrated by David Cuzik, Mark Oldroyd, David Smith
Cover illustration © Jamel Akib 2002
Repro by Digital Imaging, Glasgow
Printed in Great Britain by Ashford Colour Press, Gosport, Hants.

Notre Dame of Paris

by Victor Hugo
Adapted by Steve Barlow
and Steve Skidmore

THE BEGINNING

In 1466, a band of wandering gypsies stole the beautiful baby daughter of a woman called Paquette.
In her place, they left a four-year-old boy with a deformed face and a twisted spine.

Mad with grief, Paquette went to Paris, where she walled herself up in a tiny cell with a barred window overlooking a square near Notre Dame cathedral. Her only possession was one of her daughter's shoes, which the gypsies left behind.

Meanwhile, the boy left by the gypsies was adopted by Frollo, the Archdeacon of Notre Dame, and given the name Quasimodo. He was made bell-ringer and became strong and agile, climbing the sheer walls of the cathedral without fear. But, teased and insulted because of his deformity, he became angry and bitter. After the constant ringing of the great bells caused him to become deaf, he seldom left the cathedral.

Quasimodo

Esmerelda

Paquette

Frollo

THE STORY CONTINUES

It is now 1482, and a company of gypsies has arrived in Paris. One is a sixteen-year-old girl called Esmerelda, who entertains the crowd by dancing, while her little goat, Djali, does tricks. Archdeacon Frollo, though he hates gypsies, falls violently in love with Esmerelda. With the help of Quasimodo, Frollo tries to kidnap her. Their attempt is foiled by a poor poet, Pierre Gringoire, and Captain Phoebus of the King's bodyguard.

Following Esmerelda after her escape, Gringoire stumbles into a den of thieves. Gringoire is condemned to death as a spy by Clopin, the King of Thieves, but is rescued by Esmerelda, and he becomes her assistant.

Quasimodo is captured and sentenced to be whipped and stoned for his part in the attempt to kidnap Esmerelda. Frollo leaves his adopted son to his fate, and only Esmerelda takes pity on Quasimodo when he begs for water.

Pierre Gringoire
Captain Phoebus
Clopin
King of France

Esmerelda falls in love with the dashing, but faithless, Captain Phoebus. Frollo catches them together and, in a fit of jealous fury, stabs Phoebus and escapes. Esmerelda is blamed for Phoebus' injuries, and accused of witchcraft by Frollo. Both Esmerelda and her goat, Djali, are sentenced to death.

Frollo offers to save Esmerelda if she will love him. She refuses. As she is led to the scaffold outside Notre Dame, Quasimodo rescues her and carries her into the cathedral, claiming sanctuary. As long as she remains inside the church, she cannot be arrested.

But Frollo has decided that if he cannot have Esmerelda, no one shall. He tells Gringoire that the King of France means to break the rule of sanctuary, enter Notre Dame, and capture Esmerelda. Gringoire believes this lie and agrees to help Frollo to snatch Esmerelda.

Night falls, and so begins the final tragedy of Notre Dame of Paris.

That night, all the thieves of Paris gathered at their hideout. In their centre stood a broken barrel, from which spilled swords, axes and spears. "Come on!" The voice of Clopin, the King of Thieves, rang out above the din. "Arm yourselves!"

"Poor Esmerelda," said one of his companions. "She's our dear friend. We must get her out of Notre Dame."

"Then we must act quickly. They say the King of France has come to Paris to capture Esmerelda," said Clopin. "It is now midnight. Prepare to attack! We are an army. Keep silent and don't light your torches until we reach Notre Dame," he ordered. "We shall surprise the priests. They will run like rabbits from us. We will rescue Esmerelda!"

Inside Notre Dame, Quasimodo was not asleep.

He had climbed to the top of the North Tower and now stood gazing out over Paris. The night was very dark. The bell-ringer was uneasy. For several days now, he had seen sinister-looking men prowling round the cathedral. He wondered whether they were planning to take Esmerelda.

As Quasimodo watched, he saw a silent mob spill from the surrounding streets into the square in front of the cathedral. They came like shadows out of the mist, as silent as ghosts.

Quasimodo was terrified. Should he wake Esmerelda? No, there was no escape. Why make her suffer? He would have to defend the cathedral until help came. If help ever came at all.

Far below him, the crowd lit their torches: and the bell-ringer saw that the square was packed with men and women in rags, waving swords, axes and spears.

Clopin stepped out from the crowd. "Priests!" he cried in a voice that echoed around the square. "You have wrongly convicted Esmerelda of witchcraft. Return the girl to us, or we shall storm your cathedral, and may God help you!"

But Quasimodo was deaf and heard nothing of this speech. He believed the thieves were soldiers of the French King who had come to arrest Esmerelda.

Thirty strong men carrying hammers began to batter the doors of the cathedral. However, the doors were old and strong, and stood firm. A few moments after the attack began, a great wooden beam fell from the sky. It crushed a dozen thieves on the steps of the cathedral. The attackers fell back and looked up.

They saw no movement on the towers above them. The light of their torches did not reach so far. Superstitious muttering began. "Satan!" hissed some. "Witchcraft," whispered others, crossing themselves. They could not see Quasimodo, who had hurled the beam at them.

"Curses!" cried Clopin. "It's the priests defending themselves. Storm the cathedral!"

The mob took up the cry, and those with bows and crossbows shot blindly at the towers of the cathedral.

"We'll never get through that door," complained one of the thieves. "We need a battering ram."

"The priests have sent us one." Clopin pointed to the fallen beam.

Within moments, a hundred men were crashing the beam furiously against the door of the cathedral. The long beam and the bodies wielding it looked like a monstrous millipede, hurling itself at a stone giant. The crashes echoed inside the cathedral like the beating of a great drum, and the entire building shuddered.

At the same moment, huge stones began to rain down on the heads of the attackers. Quasimodo had discovered the rubble left by builders, who were repairing the tower. He hurled stones down on the thieves, cracking skulls left and right.

In spite of the hail of stones, the thieves kept up their attack. As the doors began to give way, the thieves yelled in triumph, and shook their fists at their invisible enemy.

Then the triumphant yells turned to screams. Two jets of molten lead were falling from the top of the cathedral. A hail of burning droplets fell on the crowd. The thieves, bellowing with pain, took to their heels.

Looking up from the edges of the square, they saw an amazing sight. Between the two great towers of Notre Dame, two hundred feet in the air, a great fire burned. Below it, on either side, two gargoyles were spewing out streams of silver rain. Above them, more gargoyles flickered in the firelight so that devils and dragons seemed to be laughing and fanning the flames. And amongst all these, they saw a moving figure.

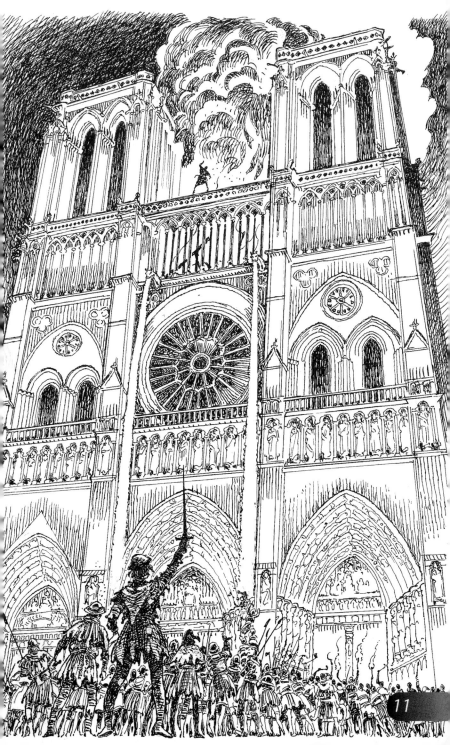

"It's that wretched bell-ringer!" said Clopin. "It's Quasimodo!"

It was indeed Quasimodo, who had built a bonfire of timber and scraps of lead left by the workmen.

Clopin shook his head and bit his fingers. "Is there no way of forcing that door?"

"Sir!" A group of thieves ran into the square carrying a long ladder. Clopin's eyes lit up. "That's the idea, lads!" He pointed to a gallery, more than sixty feet off the ground. "Get up there and into the cathedral, and you can let us through the doors."

In moments, the thieves had started to climb up to the gallery. They were led by someone carrying a crossbow. But as he reached the top of the ladder, he was confronted by the powerful figure of Quasimodo. The thief gave a cry of terror and fired his bow. The bolt went through Quasimodo's arm. The bell-ringer took no more notice than he would of a flea-bite. He wrenched the arrow out and broke it across his knee. Then he leapt for the ladder, and thrust it away with all his might. It fell to earth, smashing its load of bandits down on the stones of the pavement.

The thieves were infuriated by this defeat. They found more ladders and ropes, or climbed up the rough stones themselves, attacking the cathedral like an army of ants. They rose against Notre Dame like a living tide.

Suddenly, the sound of galloping horses echoed from the streets around the cathedral. The King of France's soldiers, led by Captain Phoebus, had arrived. Quasimodo believed the soldiers had come to help him. He prowled the gallery, throwing the attackers to their deaths.

Below him, the thieves fought with their backs against the stones of the cathedral. The fighting was terrible. Clopin cut through the soldiers with his scythe as if he were mowing a field of corn, until he was killed by a ball from a soldier's musket.

At this, the thieves fled. Quasimodo was beside himself with joy. He climbed swiftly to the room where he had left Esmerelda, to tell her he had saved her for a second time. But when he got there, the room was empty.

✳

When the thieves had begun their attack, Esmerelda had been asleep. Awakened by the noise, her first thought was that she was about to be dragged from her refuge by a mob, and hanged. She began to pray.

Then she heard footsteps behind her. Two men had entered her room. One wore a hood and carried a lantern. Esmerelda gave a cry of fear.

"Don't be afraid." The voice was one she knew. "It's me – Gringoire." The poet stroked Djali, who was butting him gently. "Your goat recognised me before you did.'

"Who is that with you?" asked the girl in a low voice.

"A friend," replied Gringoire. "Dear child, your life is in danger, and Djali's. We've come to rescue you. Come quickly!"

They went quickly down the staircase in the tower and through the cathedral, still echoing to the hammer blows of the thieves' assault. They passed through a little door that opened out onto the river. Gringoire's companion led them to a small boat and Esmerelda got in, followed by Gringoire carrying Djali. The hooded man shoved off, and rowed out over the dark water.

The current was swift and the rowing hard. Not a word was spoken as they crossed the river, away from the noise and confusion of the battle around Notre Dame. When they landed on the far bank, Esmerelda clung to Gringoire. She had begun to be afraid of the poet's silent companion.

Gringoire hugged Djali to him. "My dear Esmerelda, I can't save both of you. My friend will protect you." With these words, the poet disappeared down an alley with Djali in his arms.

In silence, and with cold hands, the hooded man led Esmerelda away. He half-dragged the frightened girl through the dark and deserted streets, until they came to the scaffold where Quasimodo had once been whipped before the crowd.

Esmerelda's guide threw back his hood, and she gave a cry of horror. The man who had led her here was Archdeacon Frollo.

The priest pointed at the scaffold. "Choose," he said in a dreadful voice. "That – or me."

A great cry arose from the other side of the river around Notre Dame. The thieves had gone, and now the 'respectable' citizens of Paris were on the streets. They were crying, "Death to the witch! Death to the gypsy girl!"

Esmerelda looked at the scaffold, then back at the priest. She said, "It doesn't horrify me as much as you do."

Frollo's face was tormented. "I have condemned my soul to hell, I spit in the face of my God! All for you!"

"It's Phoebus I love, not you!" cried Esmerelda. "He is handsome. You are old and ugly. Go away."

Frollo grabbed her. "Die, then!" He dragged her to a barred window set in a wall facing the square – the cell of the madwoman Paquette, who had been walled up in this tiny room for sixteen years nursing her grief and a hatred of all gypsies.

"Woman!" Frollo called. "Here's the gypsy! Take your revenge!"

A wasted arm came through the window and seized Esmerelda in a grip of iron.

"Don't let her go!" cried the priest. "I'll call the guard. Then you'll see her hanged!" Frollo hurried away.

"Yes, yes!" Paquette's voice was harsh and full of hate. "They'll hang you, gypsy girl!"

Esmerelda was faint with fear. "What have I done to you?"

"What have you done?" the woman shrieked. "I had a baby, a pretty little daughter. My baby was stolen by gypsies! You are a gypsy! That's what you've done to me!" She wept and gnashed her teeth.

More cries arose. "Where is the gypsy? Hang her!"

"Madame," cried Esmerelda, "do you want to see them kill me? Let me go, I beg you!"

"Give me back my baby! Gypsies stole my baby, I tell you. All I have left of her is this shoe." The crazed woman showed Esmerelda the little embroidered shoe she had kept beside her all those years.

Esmerelda stared at it. Then, with her free hand, she fumbled at the small, beaded purse which she wore around her neck, and brought out a shoe that was identical to the one in Paquette's hand.

"Dear God in Heaven," Paquette whispered, "you are my daughter." She gave a cry of joy. She hugged Esmerelda through the bars of her cell, and laughed and wept.

"Mother," cried Esmerelda, "Mother, save me. They are going to hang me!"

Suddenly, Paquette understood. She took hold of the bars at her window, and, with inhuman strength, tore them free of the stones in which they were set. Then she pulled Esmerelda through the hole.

"I shall save you!" she cried. "The Good God has given you back to me. I didn't lose you for sixteen years only to have you for just one minute. You will be safe – they are afraid of Paquette the madwoman. They will not come here … "

At that moment, soldiers with torches arrived outside the cell.

"Where is the witch?" cried one. "The Archdeacon said the madwoman had her."

Esmerelda, trembling in the darkest corner of the cell, heard a horse approaching. "Sergeant," a voice cried, "hanging witches is no job for a soldier. I'm returning to my men." It was the voice of Captain Phoebus.

Esmerelda leapt forward, and dragged herself back through the broken window. "Phoebus," she cried, "my Phoebus! Save me!"

But Phoebus had gone. As soon as he had spoken, he had wheeled his horse round and galloped away. As Esmerelda left her hiding place, she was seized by the soldiers.

"NO!" Esmerelda's mother pulled herself out of the cell. She tried to fight off the soldiers. Brutally, they flung her away from them. Her head fell heavily on the paving. She did not move again. She was dead.

Esmerelda was dragged to the scaffold.

✳

When Quasimodo had found Esmerelda's room was empty, he had run all over the cathedral looking for her in a frenzy of grief and fear. At last, he was forced to admit defeat. Esmerelda was nowhere to be found in the great cathedral. But someone else was there.

Archdeacon Frollo walked past Quasimodo without seeing him. The priest climbed the steps of the tower. The bell-ringer followed. When he emerged onto the platform on top of the tower, Quasimodo saw that Frollo was leaning over the stone rail. His eyes were fixed on the square, just the other side of the river below.

The sun was beginning to rise over the rooftops of Paris as Quasimodo stepped silently up behind Frollo. He followed the priest's gaze.

There was a crowd of soldiers and townspeople around the scaffold in the square.

 As Quasimodo watched, a man began to climb the ladder to the scaffold, carrying a woman over his shoulder. She had a noose round her neck.

Quasimodo stood as still as stone. The woman was Esmerelda.

The man reached the top of the ladder and fixed the noose to the scaffold. Then he came back down and kicked the ladder away. The girl fell.

At that moment, Frollo threw back his head and laughed the laugh of a fiend. Quasimodo could not hear the laugh but he saw it. He reached out and pushed Frollo in the back.

With a cry of despair, the priest toppled over the rail and fell, screaming, into the abyss.

The bell-ringer looked from the dead girl to the broken body of the Archdeacon lying on the stones beneath the tower, and wept.

"Oh," he cried. "All that I have loved!"

✳

Esmerelda's body was taken for burial, and Quasimodo was never seen again in Notre Dame.

That should have been the end of the story. Except that, two years after that night, workmen who broke open the tomb where Esmerelda had been laid to rest found not one, but two skeletons. One was that of a young girl. Holding it in a tight embrace was that of a man with a twisted spine. When they tried to prise him free from the skeleton in his arms, he crumbled into dust.

THE Hound OF THE Baskervilles

by Sir Arthur Conan Doyle
Adapted by Steve Barlow and Steve Skidmore

THE LEGEND *In the seventeenth century, Lord Hugo Baskerville of Baskerville Hall in Devon fell in love with a young peasant girl. However, she did not return his love, so Hugo kidnapped her and imprisoned her in Baskerville Hall. One night, whilst Hugo and his friends were drinking heavily, the girl escaped. Hugo discovered her escape and, in a drunken rage, rode after her onto Dartmoor. His companions followed, but soon came upon a terrible sight. They found Hugo lying on the ground with his throat ripped open. Standing over Hugo's body was a great black beast shaped like a hound, with blazing eyes and fire dripping from its mouth. From that day on, it was said there was a curse on the Baskerville family and all the descendants would die horrible deaths.*

THE STORY SO FAR *It is October, 1889. Sir Charles Baskerville's body has recently been discovered near the moor. Although he had a look of terror on his face, an enquiry has decided that he died of a heart attack. However, near the dead man's body were the footprints of a giant hound.*

The famous detective, Sherlock Holmes, and his friend, Dr John Watson, have been called in to investigate the death further. They learn that the title has now passed to Sir Charles' nephew, Henry Baskerville, who has been living in Canada, but has now returned to England. Sir Henry receives a warning that his life is in danger if he goes to Baskerville Hall. He ignores this and travels to Devon, accompanied by Dr Watson.

Meanwhile, Holmes travels to Dartmoor to spy on the various suspects who live on the moor. After a series of adventures, Holmes deduces that Sir Charles was murdered. His chief suspect is Stapleton, a local butterfly collector, who lives with his sister in Merripit House, on the moor. Stapleton has a secret – he is next in line to inherit the title, and he now plans to kill Sir Henry.

Holmes has set a trap for Stapleton. The bait is Sir Henry, who has agreed to visit Merripit House for supper, and then walk back alone across the moor to Baskerville Hall. Holmes, Watson and Inspector Lestrade, from Scotland Yard, are on their way to Merripit House to wait for Stapleton to make his deadly move.

The tale is told by Doctor Watson.

My nerves thrilled with anticipation as our hired carriage clattered over the dark moor track. Every stride of the horses and every turn of the wheels took us nearer to our adventure. Soon, the driver brought the horses to a halt and I jumped out of the carriage. Holmes and Lestrade followed. We paid the driver and began our walk to Merripit House.

"Are you armed, Lestrade?" asked Holmes.

The detective gave a smile. "I am always ready for emergencies."

"Good! Then we will soon put to rest the curse of the Hound of the Baskervilles."

"When did you first suspect that Sir Charles' death was a case of murder?" asked Lestrade.

"In London," replied Holmes. "Remember, Watson, when Sir Henry arrived from Canada and had a boot stolen from his hotel?"

"Yes, of course," I replied. "But how could a stolen boot be of any consequence?"

"Because only a real hound, not some supernatural creature, would need a scent. I realised that the person who caused Sir Charles' death was planning something similar for Sir Henry. All I needed to find out was who this was."

"What made you suspect Stapleton?" I asked.

"During my stay on Dartmoor, I made enquiries," answered Holmes. "I discovered that Stapleton and his sister are, in reality, man and wife."

"Married!" I exclaimed. "Why would they pretend they were brother and sister?"

"No doubt it is part of their plan," said Holmes.

"Can't we arrest them now?" I ventured.

"We don't have enough evidence yet," said Holmes. "No jury would convict Stapleton. We must catch him red-handed. This is why we are using Sir Henry, alone and unprotected, as the bait."

Lestrade glanced around at the gloomy slopes of the moor and at the huge lake of fog which lay over Grimpen Mire. "I see the lights of a house ahead of us."

"That is Merripit House, and the end of our journey," said Holmes. "I must ask you now to walk on tiptoe and not talk above a whisper."

We moved carefully along the track before Holmes stopped us about two hundred yards from the house. He pointed to a rocky hollow. "Let us wait here, ready for our ambush."

We settled down amongst the rocks, waiting for Sir Henry to leave Merripit House and take his dangerous walk back across the moor.

The fog was drifting slowly in our direction. It banked itself up like a wall – low, thick, but well defined. The moon shone on it, making it look like a great shimmering ice-field. Holmes muttered impatiently as he watched its sluggish drift. "It's moving towards us."

"Is that serious?" I asked.

"Very serious indeed – it is the one thing that could ruin my plans. Sir Henry's life may depend on his coming out of the house before the fog reaches the path."

The night was clear and fine above us. The stars shone cold and bright, and a half moon bathed the whole scene in a soft, uncertain light. Stapleton's house loomed before us, outlined against the silver-spangled sky. Broad bars of golden light from the lower windows stretched across the orchard and the moor. As we watched, one of them went out. The servants had left the kitchen. There only remained the lamp in the dining room, where the murderous host and his intended victim still chatted over their cigars.

The fog moved in. Every minute, the white woolly blanket, which already covered half of the moor, was drifting closer and closer to the house. The first thin wisps were already curling across the golden square of the lighted window.

The farthest wall of the orchard was invisible, and the trees were standing out of a swirl of white vapour. As we watched, the fog-wreaths came crawling round both corners of the house and rolled slowly into one dense bank, on which the upper floor and roof floated like a strange ship on a shadowy sea.

Holmes struck his hand on the rock in front of us and stamped his feet impatiently. "If Sir Henry isn't out in a quarter of an hour, the path across the moor will be covered. In half an hour, we won't be able to see our hands in front of our faces."

"Shall we move back onto higher ground?" I asked.

Holmes nodded. "Yes, I think it would be as well."

As the fog bank flowed onwards, we moved back until we were half a mile from the house. Still that dense white sea, with the moon silvering its upper edge, swept slowly and inexorably on.

"We are going too far," said Holmes. "We dare not take the chance of Sir Henry being overtaken before he can reach us. At all costs, we must hold our ground here."

He dropped onto his knees and clapped his ear to the ground. "Thank heaven, I think I can hear him coming."

A sound of quick steps broke the silence of the moor. Crouching among the stones, we stared intently at the silver-tipped fog bank in front of us. The steps grew louder, and through the fog, as through a curtain, stepped the man we were waiting for.

Sir Henry looked around him in surprise as he emerged from the fog into the clear, starlit night. Then he hurried swiftly along the path, passing close by us, and went up the long slope behind us. As he walked, he continually glanced over one shoulder, then the other, like a man who is ill at ease.

"Hush!" ordered Holmes. I heard the sharp click as he cocked his pistol. "Look out. It's coming."

There was a thin, crisp, continuous patter from somewhere in the heart of the fog. All three of us glared at the cloud, uncertain what horror was to break from the heart of it. I glanced at Holmes' face. He was pale but excited. His eyes shone brightly in the moonlight. Suddenly his expression changed to a rigid, fixed stare and his lips parted in amazement.

"Aaahh!" Lestrade gave a yell of terror and threw himself face down on the ground. I sprang to my feet and grasped my revolver, staring at the dreadful shape which sprang out from the depths of the fog.

It was a
hound. An enormous,
coal-black hound, but
unlike one that mortal eyes
had ever seen. Fire burst from its
mouth, its eyes glowered with a
smouldering glare and its face and sides
were outlined in flickering flame. Nothing
more savage, more appalling or more hellish
could ever be imagined. With long bounds, the
huge black creature ran past us and down the
track, following the footsteps of Sir Henry. We
were so paralysed with fear that we allowed it to
pass before we had recovered our nerve.

"Shoot!" yelled Holmes.

He and I both fired together and the creature gave a hideous howl, which showed that at least one of us had hit it. However, the nightmare hound did not pause but bounded onwards. Far away on the path we saw Sir Henry looking back, his face white in the moonlight, his hands raised in horror. He stared helplessly at the frightful being that was hunting him down. But the cry of pain from the hound had blown away our fears. If it was vulnerable, it was mortal, and if we could wound it, we could kill it.

I have never seen a man run as fast as Holmes ran that night. He took off after the hound, leaving Lestrade and me in his wake. As we flew up the track we heard scream after scream from Sir Henry, and the deep roar of the hound as it sprang upon its victim. It hurled Sir Henry to the ground and tore at his throat.

In the blink of an eye, Holmes emptied five barrels of his revolver into the creature's flank. With a howl of agony and a vicious snap in the air it rolled upon its back, pawed the air, and then fell limp on its side. Panting heavily, I stooped over it, my gun at the ready, but it was useless to press the trigger. The giant hound was dead.

Sir Henry lay inert on the ground. We hurried over to the stricken man and tore away at his collar. There was no sign of a wound.

"Thank heavens." Holmes breathed a sigh of relief. "We were just in time."

Sir Henry's eyelids flickered and he made a feeble attempt to move. Lestrade thrust his brandy-flask between the man's pale lips. Two frightened eyes soon looked up at us.

"My God!" whispered Sir Henry. "What in Heaven's name was it?"

"It's dead, whatever it is," replied Holmes. "We've ended the curse once and for all."

We stared at the creature stretched out before us. It was truly terrible in both size and strength. It appeared to be a cross between a bloodhound and a mastiff – gaunt, savage and as large as a small lioness. Even now, in the stillness of death, the huge jaws seemed to be dripping with a bluish flame and the small cruel eyes were ringed with fire. I placed my hand on the glowing muzzle, then held it up. My fingers gleamed in the darkness.

"Phosphorus," I said.

"A cunning preparation of it," said Holmes, sniffing at the dead animal. "There is no odour which might have interfered with the hound's sense of smell."

He turned to Sir Henry. "We owe you a deep apology for having exposed you to this fright. I was prepared for a hound, but not for such a creature as this. The fog also gave us little time to prepare for him."

Sir Henry shook his head. "You have saved my life."

"Having first endangered it," said Holmes. "Are you strong enough to stand?"

"Give me another mouthful of that brandy and I shall be fit for anything," he said, through chattering teeth. "What do you propose to do now?"

"Leave you here," replied Holmes. "You are not fit for further adventures tonight. If you will wait here for a while, one of us will accompany you back to the Hall."

Sir Henry tried to stagger to his feet, but he was still ghostly pale and he trembled in every limb. We helped him to a rock, where he sat shivering with his face buried in his hands.

"We must leave you now," said Holmes. "The rest of our work must be done and every moment is of importance. We have solved the mystery. Now we must capture Stapleton."

Leaving Sir Henry, we retraced our steps down the track.

"It's a thousand to one against our finding Stapleton at Merripit House," said Holmes. "The shots must have told him that the game was up."

"We were some distance away and this fog may have deadened the noise," I suggested.

Holmes shook his head. "He followed the hound to call him back – of that you may be sure. He's gone by this time, but we'll search the house and make certain."

The front door was open, so we rushed in and hurried from room to room. Holmes seized the lamp from the dining room and explored the downstairs of the house, but there was no sign of Stapleton. However, upstairs was different. We found one of the bedroom doors locked.

"There's someone in here!" cried Lestrade. "I can hear movements!"

There was a faint moaning and rustling from within the bedroom. Holmes kicked at the door and it flew open. All three of us rushed in, pistols at the ready. But there was no sign of that desperate villain. Instead, we were faced with the sight of a figure bound to a post by several sheets and towels. Two dark, terrified eyes stared back at us.

In a moment we had torn off the gag that covered the face, and loosened the bonds. Mrs Stapleton sank upon the floor in front of us. We saw the mark of a whiplash on her neck.

"The brute!" cried Holmes. "He has beaten her! Put her in the chair. Lestrade, give me your brandy-flask."

We did as Holmes instructed and he gave Mrs Stapleton a sip of brandy. Soon the poor woman opened her eyes.

"Is he safe?" she asked. "Has he escaped?"

"He cannot escape us, madam," I said defiantly. "He will answer for his deeds."

"No, I did not mean my husband. I meant Sir Henry. Is he safe?"

"Yes," Holmes nodded.

"And the hound?"

"It is dead."

Mrs Stapleton gave a long sigh of satisfaction. "Thank God! Oh, this villain! See how he has treated me!" She lifted her arms, and as her sleeves fell back we saw that they were covered with bruises.

"But this is nothing!" she cried. "It is my mind and soul he has tortured and defiled. We have lived a life of deceit." She broke into great sobs. "I thought he loved me, but now I realise that he was just using me for his own wicked plans."

"Tell us where we can find him," said Holmes.

"There is only one place he can have fled," she answered. "There is an old tin mine on an island in the middle of Grimpen Mire. It was where he kept the hound. That is where he would flee."

Holmes held the lamp to the window. The fog bank lay like white wool against it.

"No one could find his way into the mire in this," he said grimly.

She laughed and clapped her hands. Her eyes and teeth gleamed with fierce merriment. "He may find his way in, but never out. We placed marker posts to guide the way through the mire, but he will never see those tonight."

It was obvious that pursuit was impossible until the fog had lifted. Holmes instructed Lestrade to return to Sir Henry and take him back to Baskerville Hall. When the detective had gone, Holmes faced Mrs Stapleton.

"Now, madam, it is time to tell us the truth about Sir Charles' death."

Mrs Stapleton nodded sadly and began her tale. "We were living in Yorkshire when my husband discovered that he was one of the few remaining members of the Baskerville family. Only two people stood between him and the Baskerville estates and money: Sir Charles and Sir Henry. He had heard of the Baskerville legend and decided to make use of it. We moved to Dartmoor to be near Sir Charles. My husband did not want to reveal who he really was, so he forced me to pretend to be his sister and changed our names to Stapleton. He also discovered that Sir Charles suffered from a weak heart and this knowledge helped him to form his evil plan.

"My husband acquired the hound. He brought it here secretly and kept it at the mine. On the night of Sir Charles' death, my husband lured him to the edge of the moor and then set the hound upon him."

"It must have been a dreadful sight," I murmured. "That huge black creature with its flaming jaws and blazing eyes."

"Indeed," agreed Holmes. "So frightening that Sir Charles fell dead from a heart attack."

Mrs Stapleton gave a guilty sob. "Now only Sir Henry stood between my husband and the title. He had to be killed! My husband found out when Sir Henry was returning to London from Canada and travelled to the city, where he stole Sir Henry's boot."

"To give the hound Sir Henry's scent," Holmes added grimly.

Mrs Stapleton nodded. "Then when Sir Henry came down to Dartmoor, my husband made friends with him and, by pretending that I was his sister, encouraged Sir Henry to take an interest in me."

Holmes' eyes narrowed. "To make him visit this house regularly," he said. "And then, when the time was right, Stapleton would set the hound upon him, trusting that the savage beast would either kill Sir Henry or drive him into the mire."

"But I tried to stop him!" cried Mrs Stapleton. "This morning he brought the hound to the house from its refuge on the island. I said there must be no more blood on our hands and we should stop. But it was no use. The fiend beat me and then tied me up."

"It is as I deduced," nodded Holmes. "With Sir Henry's death, your husband would have made his claim for the title. It is a good job we have thwarted his evil plans."

Next morning, the fog had lifted and Mrs Stapleton guided us to the pathway at the edge of Grimpen Mire. We looked on the expanse of green-scummed pits and slimy water plants. We followed the way marked by the posts, placed by Stapleton. Even though we stayed on the pathway, the bog still gripped at our feet as if some evil spirit was trying to drag us down into its depths.

As we picked our way carefully along the treacherous path, we saw a dark object sticking out from a clump of cotton grass.

"Someone has passed this way!" exclaimed Holmes. He stepped from the path, grabbed the object, and sank to his waist. Had we not been there to haul him out, he would have surely sunk into the depths of the quagmire.

Back on dry land, he held up the object. It was a black boot. On the inside was printed 'Meyers Shoemakers, Toronto'.

"It is Sir Henry's missing boot," said Holmes. "Stapleton used it to set the hound on Sir Henry's scent, then threw it away as he fled."

"So he must have got this far," I said.

Holmes nodded. "But how much further?"

He wiped at the foul-smelling mud clinging to his trousers. "Running in that fog … " He shook his head. "This far, but no further, I think."

I shuddered at the thought of Stapleton stumbling into the mire – clutching in vain for a handhold as the bog slowly pulled him down – his screams for help muffled by the enveloping fog, as he sank deeper and deeper into the murky depths that would be his grave.

At last we reached firmer ground and found the island where the murderer had kept the hound. We found a chain, tins of phosphorus, and gnawed bones. However, there was no sign of Stapleton.

"Has he escaped then?" asked Lestrade.

"Unlikely." Holmes looked back across the huge expanse of bog. He shook his head and swept his long arm towards the dark, brooding landscape. "One of the most dangerous men we have ever hunted down is lying out there. Justice has surely been done."

Holmes turned back to me and gave a grim smile. "Come, Watson, our work here is finished. It is time for us to return to London. The case of the Hound of the Baskervilles is closed."

Great Expectations

by Charles Dickens

Adapted by Michael Lawrence

Chapter One

My first name is Philip, and my last is Pirrip, but when I was very small the best I could make of these two together was 'Pip'. So I called myself Pip, and Pip I remained, to myself and everyone else. I was the last of seven children, and the only boy to survive. My parents died, too, when I was very young, whereupon I went to live with my older sister and her husband, Joe Gargery.

We lived near the river, within twenty miles of the sea. Marsh country, it was: a dark, flat wilderness intersected by dykes and mounds and gates, with scattered cattle grazing where they could. But the bleakest part of all was the churchyard, a very neglected place, overgrown with nettles.

On a certain afternoon, as the light began to fade and a raw wind rushed in from the sea, I went alone to the churchyard to visit the dead of my family. Standing there, by my parents' headstones, and the row of tiny graves that contained my five brothers, such a mournful feeling crept upon me that I began to shiver and cry.

"Hold your noise!" cried a terrible voice.

I whirled about, fist to mouth. A fearful man had risen from among the graves. He was dressed in mud-spattered grey, with an old rag tied about his head and a great iron chain on his leg.

"Don't move, you little devil, or I'll cut your throat!" he growled. His teeth chattered with cold as he limped towards me, dragging his chain.

"Oh, don't cut my throat, sir," I pleaded in terror. "Please don't, sir."

"We'll see about that," he said. "What's your name? Quick now!"

"P–P–Pip, sir," I said.

"What? Speak clear, lad!"

"Pip, sir. My name is Pip."

"Show us where you live," he commanded. "Point it out to me!"

I pointed to where our village lay, a mile or so from the church. Then he looked at me, lifted me upside-down, and emptied my pockets. All he found was a small piece of bread I'd brought to nibble on. Turning me upright once more, he seated me on a high tombstone, where I remained, trembling, while he ate the bread ravenously.

"What fat little cheeks you got," he said when he'd finished. "Darn me if I couldn't eat them too."

My hands flew to my face. "Oh sir, please don't eat my cheeks."

He gave a short laugh. But then he scowled again. "Where's your mother?"

"There, sir!"

He started at this, and made to run, thinking my mother had come upon us. "No, sir, I mean *there*," I said, pointing at my mother's stone.

"Oh," said he, peering at it. "And is that your father alongside her?"

I told him that it was, and pointed out my five brothers too.

"Who d'ye live with then?" he asked. "Supposin' I *let* you live, which I ain't made up my mind about yet."

"My sister, sir, and her husband, Joe Gargery, the blacksmith."

"Blacksmith, eh?" said the man, glancing down at the iron on his leg. He came closer to the tombstone I was on and took me by both arms, then tilted me back so that his eyes glared fiercely down into mine, and mine looked helplessly up into his. "Now lookee here," he said. "You know what a file is?"

"Yes, sir."

"And you know what wittles is?"

"Yes, sir. Food, sir."

He tilted me further back, so as to make me feel even more helpless and afraid. "You get me a file, and you get me wittles, and you bring 'em to me or I'll have your heart and liver out. Understand me, boy?"

"Yes, sir. But if you would set me straight, I might understand even better."

He pulled me upright on top of the stone. "You see that old hut yonder?" he said.

I followed his pointing finger. The hut was nothing but a ruin, with part of the roof caved in, and no door to speak of. "Yes, sir, I see it."

"Bring that file and them wittles to me there, tomorrow morning early, and don't you say a word or make any sign that you've seen me, and you shall live. You fail, or if you let on about our little meeting, and your heart and liver shall be tore out, roasted, and ate."

"I'll bring you what you want, sir," I promised, "and I won't tell a living soul."

"Or a dead one," he said, looking about him.

"No, sir. Or a dead one."

But he wasn't yet done with his threats. "I ain't alone, as you may think I am. There's a young man with me, and compared to him I am an Angel. That young man has a way all of his own of getting at a boy. A boy may lock his door, he may draw the bedclothes over his head and think himself safe, but that young friend of mine will creep his way to him, very soft, and tear out his heart and liver. And that's what he'll do to you if you ain't here tomorrow morning, early, with a file and wittles. Or if you tell on us, too."

I assured him once again that I would get him the things he wanted, and keep everything to myself, and at last he took me down from the stone.

"Now you get off home," he said. "Go on, off with you."

"Thank you, sir," I replied. "Good night, sir."

"Good for some," he said, hugging his shivering body with both arms.

I watched him limp away, dragging his chain between the graves. When he came to the church wall he climbed stiffly over it, then set off across the marsh towards the old hut. I cast my eyes about for the horrible young man who might tear my heart and liver out, but saw no sign of him. Even so, the thought that he was hiding somewhere near set me to running all the way home without stopping.

Chapter Two

When I reached the village and ran into the house, I found Joe sitting alone in the kitchen, by the fire. "Where have you been, Pip?" he said, looking up. "Mrs Joe has been out a dozen times looking for you. She's out now, and won't be pleased when she sees you."

I shuddered at the thought of my sister's anger. She was twenty years older than me, with a hard and heavy hand which I'd felt the back of many a time.

Almost at once, we heard her returning. I looked about me in panic, but there was nowhere to hide.

"Where you been, you young monkey?" she cried, seeing me. "Tell me what you've been doing to worry me this way or I'll beat you black and blue!"

"I've only been to the churchyard," I protested.

"Churchyard indeed! You'll drive me to the churchyard one of these days, and oh, I'd like to see how you manage then!"

With this said, my sister sawed a thick round off a loaf of bread, which she sliced into two halves, of which Joe got one, and I the other. I was hungry, but I dared not eat the large piece of bread. I had to keep it, and hide it away, to take to the churchyard tomorrow for my new acquaintance and the dreadful young man who could creep into houses and whip out hearts and livers. I waited for my moment, and when Joe glanced at the fire, I pushed my hunk of bread down one of my trouser legs. I should have thought ahead, for when Joe turned back and saw that my bread was gone, with me pretending to have swallowed it whole, he was concerned.

"You oughtn't to gulp your food that way, Pip," he said, very quietly, so the mistress of the house wouldn't hear. "It could stick somewhere and do you some damage."

Suddenly the distant boom of great guns reached us on the wind. "There's another one off," said Mrs Joe from the stove.

"Another what?" I asked.

"Convict escaping," said Joe. "Two nights running now. Didn't you hear the guns last night, just after sunset?"

"Yes, but I didn't know what they were. What's a convict?"

"Why, a convict is a prisoner on the Hulks, Pip. You didn't know that either?"

I shook my head. "What's the Hulks, Joe?"

"That boy!" exclaimed my sister. "Answer him one question and he'll ask you a dozen more."

"Hulks is prison ships that you find all across the marshes," Joe told me gently.

I thought of my sorry friend in the graveyard, and said, "I wonder who's put in the prison ships, and why they're put there?"

This was too much for Mrs Joe. "People are put in the Hulks," she said angrily, "because they murder, and rob, and do all sorts of bad. And they always begin by asking questions, so you'd better watch out, my lad."

When I went up to bed (and with some relief removed the hunk of bread from my trousers) I thought how handy the Hulks were for me. I was bound to end up there, for I was already asking questions, and soon my criminal career would begin. At the first faint light of dawn I must rob the pantry for the convicts escaped from the Hulks.

Chapter Three

As soon as my window turned grey with morning, I got up and crept downstairs. I took some cheese, a meat bone, a large pork pie, and some brandy from a stone bottle. There was a door in the kitchen that led to the blacksmith's forge. I went in and found a file among Joe's tools. Then I went out and quietly closed the door after me.

It was a frosty morning, and very damp. I hurried towards the marshes. There I found the mist very thick, and had to watch my step. I had just crossed a ditch some way past the churchyard when I saw the man. He was sitting on a large stone with his back to me. He had his arms folded, and seemed to be nodding forward in sleep. I thought he would be pleased that I had brought his breakfast, so I went forward softly and touched him on the shoulder. He instantly jumped up, and turned. It was not the same man!

He was dressed in coarse grey like the other, and he too had an iron on his leg. He was rough and cold and everything the other man was, except that he had a different face. *It's the young man that cuts out hearts and livers!* I thought, a second before he swore at me and made to hit me. I ducked, so he missed me and almost lost his balance. Then he turned about, and ran off into the mist.

I soon reached the old hut after that, and found the right man just outside, hugging himself and limping to and fro. He looked deadly cold, and awfully hungry, too. Seeing the bundle I'd brought, he commanded me to open it.

"What's in the bottle?" said he.

"Brandy, sir."

He was already eating furiously, but he left off to take some of the liquor. He shivered so violently all the while that it was all he could do to keep the neck of the bottle between his teeth without biting it off.

"I think you've got a fever from lying out in the marshes," I told him.

"I think I have," said he. "I'll eat my breakfast afore it's the death of me." He was gobbling everything at once, staring distrustfully at the mist all around us, and often stopping to listen.

"You're not deceiving me?" he said. "You brought no one with you?"

"No, sir! No!"

"Well," he said, "I believe you," and he smeared his ragged sleeve over his eyes. So hungry was he that once he had started, he looked as if he would never stop until everything was gone, and I began to be concerned.

"I'm afraid you won't leave any for him," I said timidly. "There's no more to be got where that came from."

He stopped munching and looked sharply at me. "Leave any for who?"

"The young man you spoke of. Him that was hid with you."

"Oh!" he replied with a gruff laugh. "I was pulling your leg. There's no other."

"But I've seen him," I said in surprise.

He stopped eating and looked keenly at me. "Seen him? Seen who?"

"The one I thought was your friend. I took him for you at first. He was dressed like you, only with a hat."

"This man," he said slowly. "Was there anything about his face?"

"Yes, he had a large birthmark." I touched my cheek to show him. "Right here."

"So he got out too, curse him." He spat on the cold ground, then crammed what little food was left into his grey jacket. "Well, I'll find him. I'll pull him down like a bloodhound. Did you bring that file, like I told you to?"

"Yes, sir." I took the file from my coat and at once he was down in the wet grass, filing at his leg iron like a madman. I was still very much afraid of him, but I was also afraid of being away from home any longer. "I must go," I said. "Mrs Joe will miss me, and I'll be in trouble."

He took no notice, just filed fiercely at his iron, so I slipped away.

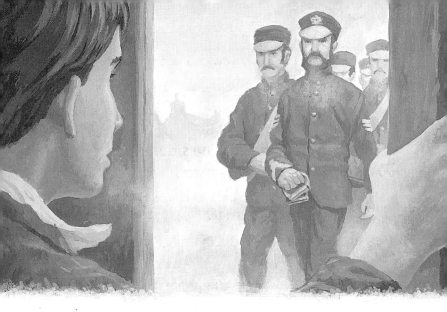

Chapter Four

In fact, Mrs Joe hadn't missed me at all. She hadn't missed the wittles I'd stolen yet either, but she would sooner or later, so I kept an eye on her, so as to be ready. When I heard her open the pantry, I panicked and ran for the door. I got no further than that, however, for when I opened it I found a party of soldiers approaching, led by a sergeant holding out a pair of handcuffs. I was caught! My crime had been discovered after all! I was to be carted off to the Hulks!

At that very moment Mrs Joe returned from the pantry, saying, "The pie has gone! My lovely pork pie that we was to have for dinner. We've been robbed!" But then she saw the soldiers, and stopped short.

"Excuse me, madam," said the sergeant, "but I've come for the blacksmith."

"Pray what has my Joe done that you want him so badly?" my sister said.

"I know nothing of what he's done," the sergeant replied. "I need him to fix the lock of this pair of handcuffs, which is broken."

Mrs Joe called her husband, who came in from the workshop, where he'd been lighting the forge. He looked the handcuffs over and announced that it would take about two hours to mend them.

"Then kindly set about it at once," the sergeant said. "My men will wait here."

I observed all this with relief. Not only were the handcuffs not for me, but the appearance of the soldiers had driven all thought of the missing pie from my sister's mind.

"How far are we from the marshes here?" the sergeant enquired as his men trooped into the warm and piled their muskets in a corner.

"Just a mile," said Mrs Joe.

"Good. No distance. We'll catch them in no time."

"Escaped convicts, sergeant?" asked Joe.

"Aye, two. They're out on the marshes somewhere. They won't get far."

When Joe's work was done, it was he who proposed that he and I go with the soldiers and see what came of the hunt. To my surprise, Mrs Joe agreed to let me go, but she made one warning to Joe. "If you bring the boy home with his head blown to bits by a musket, don't look to me to put it together again."

The soldiers fell in, and Joe and I received orders (from the sergeant, not my sister) to keep to the rear and speak no word after we reached the marshes. And so we set off. When we reached the churchyard, the sergeant sent some of his men to search among the graves. They returned having found nothing, and we struck out across the open marshes. A bitter sleet rattled against us, and Joe took me up on his back.

Now that we were out upon the dismal wilderness where I had so recently seen both men hiding, I considered what might happen if we came upon them. Would my particular convict suppose that it was I who had brought the soldiers after him? Would he think I had betrayed him? With thumping heart, I looked about from Joe's broad shoulders for any sign of the pair. I saw none. But all of a sudden we heard a great shout a little to the east.

The shout was repeated, and followed by another. The sergeant ordered his men to make towards the shouts at the double, and silently. So we all started eastward, at a run. The shouting continued, growing louder, as we went. And then the sergeant and the first of his men jumped down into a ditch, and he cried, "Here they are, both of them! Surrender, you two! Surrender!"

Water was splashing, and mud was flying, and we heard blows being struck as we drew near, and there was much more shouting. More soldiers went down into the ditch to help the sergeant, and between them they dragged out my convict and the other one. Both were bleeding and panting and struggling.

"It was me that took him!" my convict said, wiping blood from his face with a ragged sleeve. "I was the one that give him up to you! Mark that!"

"It'll do you little good, being in the same plight yourself," the sergeant said, and he ordered his men to handcuff the desperadoes.

"I don't expect it to do me any good," my convict said. "I just want it known – I want *him* to know – that it was me that took him."

The other convict, clearly his deadly enemy, was furious. "He tried to murder me!" he shouted. It looked that way too. In addition to the large birthmark on the side of his face, he seemed to be cut and bruised all over.

But my convict merely laughed. "What I done was prevent him getting off the marshes. He's an evil one, and I brought him down for you. I want it known."

As he said this, he saw me for the first time. I had got down from Joe's back at the top of the ditch and had been waiting for the man to see me. When I had his eye, I moved my hands slightly and shook my head, to show that it was not I who had brought the soldiers here. He gave no sign of recognising me.

"All right," the sergeant said when both men were secure. "March!"

The two were kept apart, and each walked accompanied by a guard. Soon we came to a rough wooden hut and a landing place by the water. There were guards in the hut, and we joined them to warm ourselves by the fire. The second convict was taken away first, to the prison ship nearby. My man didn't look at me again, but while he stood waiting for the guards to come back and take him, he turned to the sergeant and said, "I want to say something about my escape, so that no one else gets blamed. I was hungry, and I took some wittles up at the village yonder. I stole them from the blacksmith's. There was a pie, and some other things."

The sergeant turned to Joe. "Have you missed such articles, blacksmith?"

"My wife did," said he, "at the very moment you came in."

I stared at the convict, trying to understand why he should take my blame. The convict turned to Joe, without the least glance my way. "So you're the blacksmith? Then I'm sorry to say, I've eaten your pie."

"You're welcome to it," said Joe. "We don't know what you've done, but we wouldn't have you starved to death for it – would we, Pip?"

I shook my head and looked into the convict's eyes as they turned to me. He nodded briefly, in a secret sort of way. Then the guards returned and escorted him onto the dark prison boat. I watched him go, thinking that he had no future, no future at all, and vowed that whatever I made of my life I would never do anything that would bring me to a place like this. My expectations of the life ahead of me were suddenly very great. Very great indeed.